Disney
PRINCESS

Magical Moments

kids publications international, ltd.

Cinderella just loves the dress her little friends have made for her! Can you spot some of their other creations spread throughout the room?

Little black dress

Lambswool dress

Mohair dress

A-line dress

Ball gown

Tiana wants to run her very own restaurant. But for now, she is working toward her dream by waitressing at Duke's Diner. As she heads into work, can you find these examples of New Orleans cuisine on Claiborne Street?

Pecan pie

King cake

Beignets

Pralines

Muffuletta

Jambalaya

Crawfish

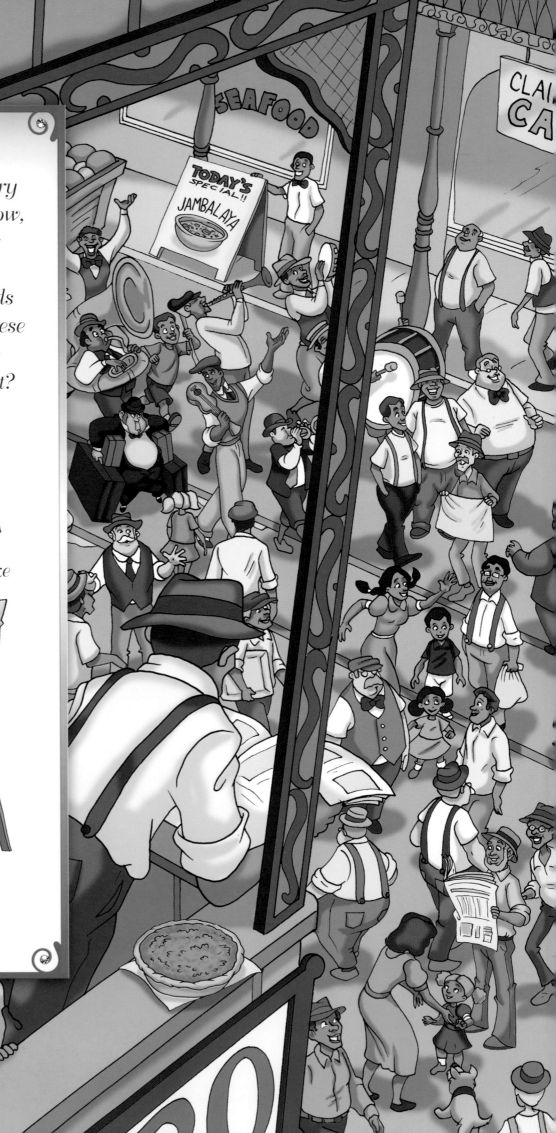

Lumiere, Mrs. Potts, and all the other enchanted objects want Belle to feel at home. Among all the snacks and desserts, there are a few unusual things she hasn't seen before. Can you find them?

French bread

Angel food cake

Caesar salad

Chilled asparagus

Strawberry shortcake

Aged cheese

Chicken à la king

Ariel loves exploring sunken ships and searching for treasures from the human world. Now it's your turn to look around. Can you find these fancy fish swimming about the ship?

Crowned cod

Sapphire bluegill

Ruby-red snapper

Goldfish

Silver swordfish

At midnight, Cinderella will lose a glass slipper. But some other maidens at the ball have already lost their accessories! Can you help these ladies find what they have misplaced?

Her earring

Her cape

Her fan

Her glove

Her necklace

Her purse

Tiana and Naveen are human again...and married! As they prepare to celebrate their happily ever after, look around for these delighted guests.

Louis

Mama Odie

Eudora

Charlotte

Queen

Big Daddy

King

Despite the cold weather, even the birds can't help but notice that Belle is warming up to the Beast. Besides your scarf and mittens, you'll need bird-watching binoculars to find these feathered friends.

Red-headed robin

Hummingbird duet

Love birds

Bald eagle

Bluebird of happiness

Ariel and Eric are married! It was a celebration like none ever seen on land or under the sea! Look at all the friends and family members who came to wish Eric and Ariel a happy ever after.

King Triton

Carlotta

Scuttle

Grimsby

Chef Louie

Flounder

Sebastian

Max

Cinderella's friends have an eye for fashion, but when it comes to a ball, not everything goes! Go back and search the attic for these things one should NOT wear to such a fancy occasion.

- ♥ Chef's hat
- ♥ Artist's beret
- ♥ Bloomers
- ♥ Hoop skirt
- ♥ Riding boots

Catch the streetcar back to Claiborne Street and say hello to these people Tiana passed on her way to Duke's Diner.

Take another look at Belle's supper. Can you find these foods from famous sayings?

- ♥ A bowl of cherries
- ♥ Spilled milk
- ♥ A flat pancake
- ♥ A cool cucumber
- ♥ A crumbling cookie
- ♥ A hat with a bite out of it
- ♥ A pickle
- ♥ Sour grapes

It takes a long time for an oyster to make a pearl. Swim back through the sunken ship to spot these pearly pieces that have come back to the sea.

- ♥ Pearl earrings
- ♥ Pearl ring
- ♥ Pearl bracelet
- ♥ Pearl brooch
- ♥ String of pearls

*Hurry!
It's almost midnight!
Go back to the
ballroom and
find nine
timepieces.*

*Jackson Square
is always filled with
artists. Can you find
these paintings amidst
the wedding celebration?*

*No two snowflakes
are exactly alike ...
or are they? Find seven
matching pairs of snowflakes.*

*Wedding bells are
ringing over land and sea
for Ariel and Eric! Can you find
these other "bells" at their wedding?*

♥ *Barbells*
♥ *A Southern belle*
♥ *Bell-bottoms*
♥ *A bell pepper*
♥ *A belly flop*
♥ *A blue bell*